Penguin
Cha-Cha

For my Ciana. May you dance with true joy. (Psalm 150)

ISBN 978-0-545-83599-2

Published by Scholastic Inc., 557 Broadway, New York, NY 10012,
by arrangement with Random House Children's Books, a division of
Random House LLC.

12 11 10 9 8 7 6 5 4 3 2 15 16 17 18 19 20/0

Printed in the U.S.A. 40

First Scholastic printing, January 2015

Kristi Valiant

SCHOLASTIC INC.

Julia was wild about everything at the Romping Chomping Park and Zoo, especially the shows. Every weekend, she shimmied up a tall tree and watched the performance.

One Saturday, dancers moved and grooved, whirled and twirled, hip-hopped and boogie-bopped.

When a dancer tossed her feather boa backstage, Julia noticed a sneaky flipper snatch it in midair. Penguins pounced on hats and clothes, fans and bows.

Just what are those fishy penguins up to? Julia wondered.

So Julia followed the penguins as they waddled and toddled away.
HiPPO
COVE

When she got to the Penguin Cove, she peeked inside. The penguins stared back at her. Julia saw no hats. No clothes. No fans. No bows.

Just what are those fishy penguins up to? Julia wondered.

Y
E

So Julia spied on the penguins from way up high. Were they moving and grooving? Whirling and twirling? Hip-hopping and boogie-bopping? Yes! The penguins were dancing!

She couldn't believe it! She had to tell someone.

"Dancing penguins, you say? Nonsense!" said the zookeeper. "Penguins can't hip and hop and boogie and bop. Why don't you go and take another look-see."

Julia grabbed a top hat and ran to join the jazzy jitterbug.

She bounded into the Penguin Cove and shouted, "Let's dance!"

The penguins didn't flap a flipper.

They didn't shake a tail feather.

They froze like penguin Popsicles.

But when no one was around,
the penguins were having a toe-tapping,
knee-knocking, rocking good time.

Julia hatched a plan.

She would turn
herself into a penguin!

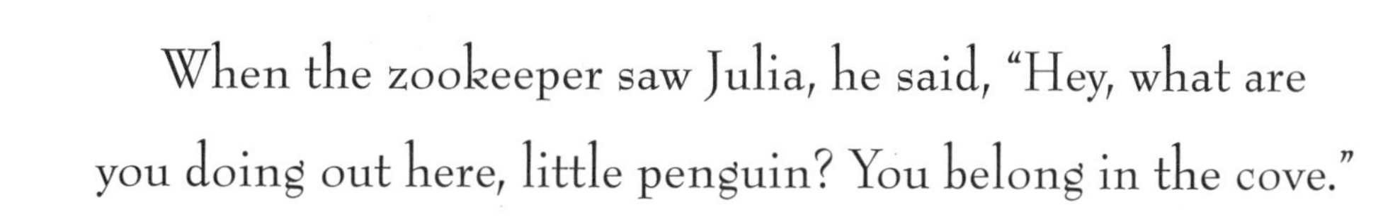

When the zookeeper saw Julia, he said, "Hey, what are
you doing out here, little penguin? You belong in the cove."

Julia wiggled and wobbled into the Penguin Cove. The penguins stared and glared but still wouldn't share a dance.

I know what I need, Julia decided.

A dance partner!

Hippo agreed to play the part.

Julia and Hippo

tangoed and fandangoed,

hustled and bustled,

and wove all over the cove!

Still, the penguins didn't budge.

Thanks for
the dance.
-Julia

Julia trudged home.

The next day, Julia returned for one last try.

"Okay, I know you won't let me join your jitterbug," Julia said to the penguins. "But may I please show you the cha-cha?"

Step,
step,
cha-cha-cha.

Step,
step,
cha-cha-cha.

Julia clapped, cha-cha-cha.

Julia snapped, cha-cha-cha.

Julia spun, cha-cha-cha.

Julia swung, cha-cha-cha.

And suddenly she heard . . .

Tap,
flap,
cha-cha-cha.

Tap,
flap,
cha-cha-cha.

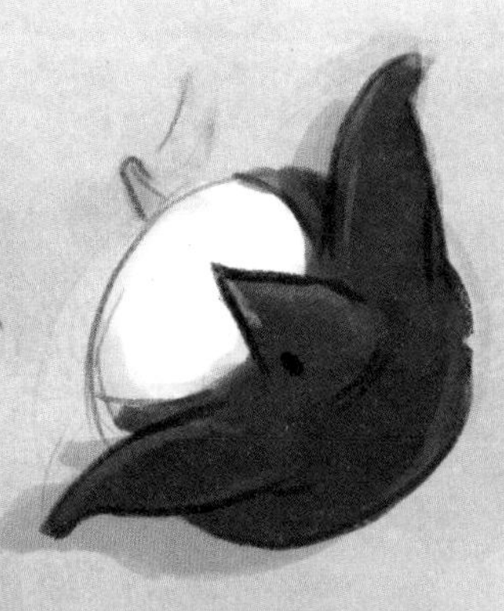

The penguins couldn't resist!
Tap, flap, cha-cha-cha.
They danced with Julia all day long!

From then on, Julia always kept her penguin costume handy.

Whenever the zookeeper checked on them, all he saw was a group of penguins, frozen like penguin Popsicles.

The next Saturday at the magic show, Julia noticed sneaky little paws swipe the magician's hat and wand.

Now, what are those tricky monkeys up to? she wondered.